By

# Justine St. John

Interior and Cover Illustrations: Randy Jennings
Interior Layout: Dianne Leonetti
Editorial and Proofreading: Eden Rivers Editorial Services
Photo Credits: Kim Rosen, Founder of Photos for Cures,
benefitting St. Jude Children's Research Hospital.
www.photosforcures.com

Published by Sweet Dreams Publishing of Massachusetts
36 Captain's Way
East Bridgewater, MA 02333

For more information about this book contact Lisa Akoury-Ross at Sweet Dreams Publishing
of MA by email at lross@PublishAtSweetDreams.com.

Sweet Dreams Publishing of MA
Permissions Department
36 Captain's Way, East Bridgewater, MA 02333
or email your request to info@PublishAtSweetDreams.com.

Library of Congress Control Number: 2011944364

ISBN-13: 978-0-9829256-3-8

Printed in the United States of America

# Acknowledgments

There are so many people to thank for helping to bring this book to life. I would like to start with my publisher Lisa Akoury-Ross. She has kept everything running smoothly, used her expertise to help guide me through this process, and has made it seem almost easy! Lisa Schleipfer, my editor, did an excellent job catching errors I never would have, made helpful suggestions, and kept a great sense of humor throughout the past few months. My illustrator, Randy Jennings, is such a talented artist, I consider myself lucky that Lisa found him for me. He took my vague ideas of what a dragon at a farmers' market would look like, and brought them to life. Dianne Leonetti worked very hard on the overall layout, and I appreciate all she has done to finalize this.

I also am eternally grateful to Jen Gershman, for taking the time to talk to me about her many positive experiences with Sweet Dreams Publishing, and encouraging me to give it a try. Without her, this would still be something I wrote for "someday."

I would like to thank Heather S., who looked at this manuscript at its earliest stage and gave me honest and encouraging feedback.

To Denise D. and Courtney L., you listened to me during this process, gave great advice, and were a great support. Thank you so much!

Also, thank you to Susie I., who was very helpful when asked to review the book for me!

Finally, I need to say a special thank you to my family. Your unwavering support and belief pushes me to be my best. I am thankful to you all.

To Art, without your love and support,
this still would be just a dream.

To Emily and Zachary, this book was imagined
because of your love of stories and reading.
Thank you for your inspiration—I love you!

Once upon a time,
there was a dragon named Wilbur.
Wilbur was just like any other dragon, except . . .
Wilbur LOVED zucchini! He even looked like a big
zucchini, tall and skinny on top, round on the
bottom, with a long green tail.

Each day, he would walk to the local farmers' market. He loved it there. There were always different and interesting people around, selling all kinds of things: ripe, red tomatoes; crunchy, green broccoli; and even funny-shaped, purple eggplant. But, Wilbur only had eyes for one thing—zucchini. There was one stand at the market that sold zucchini: Farmer Ted's.

FRESH
FLOWERS

Wilbur would buy a bushel of zucchini every day. And every day, Farmer Ted would ask if Wilbur wanted anything else. There was fresh-baked bread, yummy honey, and even homemade, nutty granola. Each day Wilbur replied, "No thank you, Farmer Ted, just zucchini." He became known to everyone at the market as Wilbur, The Zucchini-Eating Dragon.

One morning, Wilbur arrived to find Farmer Ted looking very sad. "What's wrong, Farmer Ted?" Wilbur asked. Farmer Ted explained that the shipment of zucchini he was getting from another farm was late, so he had no zucchini for Wilbur.

FRESH ZUCCHINI

"What am I going to eat?" Wilbur asked. He loved anything that had zucchini in it: zucchini parmesan, fried zucchini sticks, even just plain, roasted zucchini. In fact, he didn't know how to cook anything else but zucchini.

Suddenly, Farmer Ted had an idea. "Wilbur," he said, "I have a beautiful bushel of butternut squash I would love for you to try." Wilbur looked at the odd-shaped vegetable and scrunched up his nose. "Ewww . . . squash," he whined.

Farmer Ted pushed his straw hat back from his brow. "Now Wilbur," he said with a chuckle, "zucchini is a type of squash too, and you love that. I'll tell you what. If you take the butternut squash home and try it, I promise when you come back tomorrow I will give you a big bushel of zucchini for free. All you have to do is try the squash."

Wilbur looked at Farmer Ted. He didn't want to try the squash. He never wanted to try anything new. "Besides," he thought, "the butternut squash just looks strange. But, I would love another bushel of zucchini. And, if I don't do this, what am I going to have for dinner tonight?"

"OK," Wilbur sighed.
"I will try it." And off he went
with his bushel of squash.

That night, there was a knock on the door.
It was Wilbur's best friend Wilma. Wilma was a beautiful
purple dragon, who always was friendly and nice to others.
More importantly, she loved zucchini almost as much as Wilbur
did. They shared their dinner almost every night, laughing and
talking about things that happened to them during the day.

"So, what kind of zucchini are we having tonight?" Wilma asked.

"We are having butternut squash tonight," replied Wilbur.

"Ewww . . . SQUASH?" Wilma wrinkled her nose.

"Farmer Ted was out of zucchini, so he gave me this to try instead," said Wilbur. He had put it in the oven and roasted it, just like he would have with the zucchini. However, he had to peel the squash, cut it, scoop out the seeds, which were icky, and then finally put it in the oven. This was definitely much more work than cooking his old, reliable zucchini!

Wilma and Wilbur sat down for dinner.
Wilbur looked at Wilma and said, "Well, are you going to try
it?" Wilma shook her head. She was an adventurous dragon,
but this was a little too much. "Not me," she said, "you first."

"OK," Wilbur sighed. He stuck his fork into the steaming orange
squash in front of him. It looked nothing like the zucchini he
loved. He took a little taste. The bite was so little he didn't
actually taste anything. Wilma laughed at him.
"You have to take a bigger bite than that!" she said.

Wilbur took a larger bite. It . . . was . . . REALLY GOOD! He looked up at Wilma and said, "You have to try this—it is so yummy!" Wilma watched him for a minute and then took her own little bite, and then a bigger one. Pretty soon they both had cleaned their plates.

The next day, both Wilma and Wilbur walked to the farmers' market down the street. They passed people selling fresh flowers. They passed people giving demonstrations on how to cook with the fresh vegetables and fruits. They even passed vendors selling handmade soaps and perfumes. There was so much to do and see at the farmers' market!

Finally, they arrived at Farmer Ted's stand.
Farmer Ted looked up and smiled. "So," he said, "did you like
the squash?" Wilbur replied, "I didn't like the squash,
Farmer Ted, I LOVED it!" Farmer Ted laughed.
"I'm so glad, Wilbur! See? It can be kind of exciting trying
new things. Now, let me get that bushel of
zucchini I promised you."

Wilbur looked around at all the different colorful fruits and vegetables at Farmer Ted's stand. He looked at Farmer Ted and said, "Thank you for the zucchini, but I think I would like to try another new vegetable tonight. What would you recommend?" Wilbur asked eagerly. Farmer Ted grinned. "Well, we have some fresh broccoli, just picked this morning," he replied. "Perfect!" Wilbur cried.

From that day on, every day he arrived at the farmers' market, Wilbur was known as The Dragon That Ate All Kinds of Vegetables.

THE END

**Justine St. John** is a Westfield State College graduate and works in criminal justice, when she is not busy reading stories to her children. This book was imagined during a camping trip when there were no books to be found, and quickly became her children's favorite. Justine lives in Metrowest, Massachusetts with her husband, Arthur, son, Zachary, and daughter, Emily.

CPSIA information can be obtained
at www.ICGtesting.com
Printed in the USA
BVOW10s1845300316

442358BV00030B/285/P